# The Curious Kitten

# Other titles by Holly Webb

# The Curious Kitten

Holly Webb
Illustrated by Sophy Williams

For Ge

www.h

STRIPES PUBLISHING
An imprint of Little Tiger Press
1 The Coda Centre, 189 Munster Road,
London SW6 6AW

A paperback original
First published in Great Britain in 2016

Text copyright © Holly Webb, 2016
Illustrations copyright © Sophy Williams, 2016
Author photograph copyright © Nigel Bird
*My Naughty Little Puppy* illustration copyright © Kate Pankhurst

ISBN: 978-1-84715-661-7

A CIP catalogue record for this book is available
from the British Library.

Printed and bound in the UK.

10 9 8 7 6 5 4 3 2 1

# Chapter One

Amber rolled the jingly cat ball down the length of the hallway and giggled as Cleo flung herself after it, her paws slipping on the wooden floor. She loved the way the kitten took chasing the ball so seriously!

Her mum opened the kitchen door and gasped as she almost tripped over the skidding kitten. "Oh, Cleo!

I nearly kicked you. Are you all right?"

But Cleo didn't even seem to have noticed. She had finally caught her jingly ball and was rolling over and over with it, growling fierce kitten growls.

"I don't think that ball's coming out alive," Mum commented, smiling. "Amber, did you finish sorting out all your new pencils and things for school? Have you packed them in your rucksack?"

Amber nodded. "Everything's ready." She got up, looking worriedly between Mum and Cleo. "Mum, what's going to happen to Cleo while

I'm at school?"

"What do you mean, what's going to happen to her?" Mum looked confused.

"I'm worried she's going to be bored," Amber explained. "She's not really been on her own that much, has she?"

Amber's family had got Cleo from a local cat shelter right at the beginning of the summer holidays. Amber had been desperate to get a kitten for ages, and her parents had finally agreed. Mum and Dad and her big sister, Sara, had spent ages sitting with her on the sofa, looking at the website. But as soon as Amber had seen the photo of Cleo with her brothers and sisters, Amber had known that she was the one. Amber never seen such a gorgeous cat. Cleo was a really unusual colour –

mostly ginger, but with big dark patches and huge black ears that looked like she needed to grow into them.

Amber had spent the whole holiday playing with Cleo – it was amazing how many mad games a kitten could invent to play with just a piece of string. Or a feather. Or even the flowers on Amber's flip-flops. She was going to miss Cleo so much – and she had a feeling Cleo was going to miss her, too. Even though Cleo was officially a family cat, and everyone played with her, Amber did most of the looking after. She loved feeding Cleo and making sure she always had clean water – it made her feel that the kitten was just a little bit more hers.

"She's always had me and Sara at

home to play with," Amber went on.

"I see what you mean." Mum gave her a hug. "She'll be fine, Amber. Cats are quite independent, you know. And think how much time Cleo spends snoozing! She'll just save up her playtime for when we're all home. Anyway, I'll be around some of the time – you know I only do half days. Cleo can distract me from all the marking I've got to do!"

"I suppose so," Amber agreed, a bit doubtfully. Cleo did sleep a lot. She was still only small, and she didn't seem to understand taking things easy. She'd race around until she was exhausted and then collapse in a little furry tortoiseshell heap. Amber loved it when she flumped down with her paws in the air!

She wriggled the ball out from between Cleo's paws and rolled it back down the hallway again. "I'm worried that she'll be bored and find a way to get round the front of the house. She thinks the front garden must be the most exciting thing ever, just because we won't let her go out there. She nearly escaped again yesterday, when the postman brought that parcel."

Her mum made a face. "I honestly don't think we can do much about that. We'll just have to make sure she doesn't slip out. I think the noise of the cars would put her off going on the road anyway."

Mum didn't look all that sure, though, and Amber sighed. One of their neighbours had a cat who'd been run over and badly hurt, and she hated to think of anything like that happening to Cleo. She was sure Cleo was very clever, but kittens weren't known for being sensible. If Cleo saw something interesting on the other side of the road, Amber was almost certain she'd chase after it. And it wasn't as if she could train Cleo to look both ways first.

Cleo sniffed curiously at the bags in the hallway. Today felt different. Everyone was rushing around. She whisked behind one of the rucksacks as Sara came dashing past and nearly stepped on her tail. She crouched there, watching as Amber and Sara chased up and down the stairs, looking for things they'd forgotten. Their mum was standing in the hallway, glancing at her watch.

"Come on, you two! I thought you said you'd got everything ready last night? We really do need to go – I've got a staff meeting before school."

"I'm here, I'm ready." Amber jumped down the last two steps and looked around for her bag and shoes. "I just wanted to find a photo of Cleo to show my friends. Hardly anyone's seen her yet – only Maisie and Lila when they came over."

"I'm ready, too," Sara said, sighing. "I can't believe we're going back to school – it feels as if the holidays have only just started. And everyone says Year Eight means loads more homework." Sara's secondary school wasn't that far from the house, but she usually got a lift with Mum and Amber in the mornings and walked back home with her friends.

"I shouldn't think anyone will give you much on the first day," her mum replied. "Come on. Grab your stuff and let's get in the car."

Cleo opened her mouth in a silent mew of surprise as the bag in front of her disappeared. And then she realized – the front door was open!

"Oh, Cleo, no! Sara, stop her!" Amber called out. She was all mixed up with her PE bag and rucksack and she still only had one shoe on.

Sara crouched down to try and field the kitten, but Cleo jinked expertly around her reaching hands and skipped out on to the doorstep.

Cleo caught the different outdoor smells as she leaped down the step and then darted off to investigate the wheelie bins. She'd only managed to get out into the front garden a couple of times, and she wanted to explore.

"Did you get her?" Amber came

hurrying up to her sister.

"No, she was just too speedy!" Sara gasped. "Sorry! I think she's gone behind the bins. Here, Cleo! Come on… Puss, puss!"

Mum sighed. "How does she know when we're in a hurry? Amber, can you catch her? Try not to let her go under the car – it'll take ages to get her back out again."

Amber crouched down beside the bins. The kitten was in the flower bed now, peering out through the pink geraniums.

Cleo gazed up at her with round green eyes. She didn't understand why they made such a fuss about her being *here*, when no one minded if she went through her cat flap into the back garden. She looked around, eyeing the pavement and the road beyond. There were interesting smells out there – more cats and other things, too. But the cars speeding past were so loud that she'd never dared to do more than peek round the edge of the garden wall. She wanted to, though. She was working up to it.

"There!" Amber reached through the flowers and grabbed her, and Cleo snuggled up against her school cardigan. The kitten didn't mind being caught, not really. Especially because Amber always gave her cat treats when she brought her back in.

Cleo dived out of the cat flap and shook her ears crossly. She didn't like the way it banged behind her – it always made her feel jumpy. She licked at the fur on her white front until she felt calmer and then strolled out on to the patio. The garden was very bright, and there were fat bees blundering through the lavender bush. She could even hear a bird rustling in the apple tree at the far end. But somehow the back garden didn't seem quite as exciting as it usually did.

Cleo sat on the patio, feeling the warm afternoon sun on her fur and wondering what to do. She had slept for a lot of the morning, and now she wanted to play. Amber's mum was working on her computer, and she'd stroked Cleo for a bit. But when Cleo had tried to pounce on her keyboard, she'd shooed her away. Cleo was used to playing with Amber, and she missed her. It wasn't as much fun being on her own. She could chase down the garden after that bird or wriggle into the lavender and swipe at the bees. But she never seemed to catch anything… When would Amber come back?

Then her ears flattened and she sprang up, stalking across the patio to the bench by the garden wall. Amber had gone out of the front door. Perhaps she was at the front of the house somewhere. If she hopped up on to the bench, she wouldn't be that far from the top of the wall…

Cleo wriggled her bottom and

leaped, scrambling from the arm of
the bench into the twiggy mass of
jasmine that was growing up the wall.
She clawed and scrabbled and pulled
her way up on to the top. Half her fur
was standing on end and it was full of
tiny green leaves, but she had done it.
She was almost sure this wall led
round to the front of the house, where
Amber was.

Cleo paced
along the top
of the wall,
then over
the flat roof
of the garage.
She dropped back
down on to the wall again where it ran
along the side of the little front garden.

She had to pick her way carefully through the tall plants that grew up against it, but eventually she reached the front of the garden, where the wall was lower and half-hidden by bushes. She perched between the bushes, looking out on to the street.

"Cleo!"

The kitten peered curiously round the bushes and saw Amber racing down the street towards her, with her rucksack bouncing against her shoulders. Cleo stood up and purred, arching her back proudly. She'd been right! Amber *was* here! Amber would see that she'd been clever and climbed the wall. As Amber ran up to her, Cleo purred even louder and leaned down to rub her head against Amber's shoulder.

"Oh, Cleo," she murmured lovingly, "you're so naughty! How did you get out here? Mum, look!"

"Cleo!" Amber's mum stared at the kitten. "I made absolutely sure she didn't slip past me when I left to get you from school. She was in the house this afternoon – I know she was. She tried to sit on the computer while I was working."

Amber gently scooped the little kitten off the top of the wall. She held Cleo against her shoulder as Mum went to unlock the front door. "But that means she must have got round the house by herself," Amber said, looking up at the garden wall. "She can't have done… That wall's so high for her to jump up to, and then she had to get on to the garage roof!"

Cleo looked up at the wall, too, and purred smugly into Amber's ear.

# Chapter Two

Now that Cleo had worked out how to climb the wall in the back garden, she was desperate to try it again. Amber had homework to do – which she thought was really unfair on her first day back. She left Cleo gobbling down her tea, hoping she would come and find her when she'd finished. But Cleo had other ideas, and when Amber's dad came home from work he was met by a purring kitten on the path.

Dad laughed as Cleo danced happily around his feet and he crouched down to fuss over her. "You're not meant to be out here, little miss. Did you slip out? Come on, then."

He opened the front door and called out, "Look who I found!"

Amber and Sara peered over the top of the stairs.

"Oh no! Was she out at the front again?" Amber hurried down to scoop Cleo up. "She's definitely learned to climb the wall, then. Mum said she must have done it earlier, but I thought Cleo might have sneaked out without her noticing. She was on the front wall when I came home!"

"She was only in the front garden." Dad looked round at Amber as he hung up his jacket. "I don't think she'll come to any harm."

"What about the road, though?" Amber sighed worriedly and then laughed as Cleo's head butted into her chin. "Oh, Cleo, are you telling me not to fuss?"

"How's Cleo?" Amber's friend Maisie asked in class a couple of days later, spotting the photo that Amber had stuck on the front of her planner. "Has she learned any more tricks?" Amber had told her about all the games she'd invented with Cleo.

Amber rolled her eyes. "Yes! She's learned how to scramble on to the back wall, then climb all the way over the garage roof so she can get into the front garden."

Lila leaned over the table. "Why? What's so exciting about your front garden?"

"Who knows?" Amber sighed. "But it's got a road in front of it, that's the problem. There's this really nice lady who lives down our street, Susan. Her cat got run over last year. He crawled back in through the cat flap with a broken leg. He had to have an operation to fix the bone back together with metal pins. Then he had to live in a cat crate for two months to stop him walking on it."

"But that's not going to happen to Cleo," Lila said comfortingly.

"It might do." Amber ran her finger over Cleo's whiskers in the photo – they were so white, and they fanned out like she had a moustache. "She's only little and she doesn't know what cars are. The people across the road are starting to have an extension built this week. Mum was telling me. She was saying it might be tricky to get out of our driveway because of all the builders' vans and things. So that's loads more traffic to worry about."

"I'm sure it will be OK…" put in a quiet voice.

Amber looked over at the other side of the table, a bit surprised. The two classes in the year had been mixed around again, and she didn't know George very well. He'd always been in the other class in her year. She'd not seen him on her way to school, either, so she guessed he didn't live very close by. They'd been on the same table for a week now, but George hadn't said much at all.

"My mum's cat, Pirate, goes up and down our street, and he does cross the road sometimes. But he's really careful. I bet your kitten will just learn what to do."

"George is right," Lila agreed. "Cats are clever. I'm sure Cleo will learn how to cross the road, no problem."

"Maybe," Amber said. She loved how Cleo was so curious – it made her even more fun to play with. But it also meant that she liked to explore everything. She sighed to herself as Mr Evans told them to stop chatting and settle down. She was probably worrying too much – it was the first time they'd had a pet, after all. She just couldn't help that little nagging feeling that Cleo was too nosy for her own good.

Cleo sat perched on the front wall, peering out from under a climbing rose and eyeing the men working on the other side of the road. There was one big truck, with a crane lifting off huge pallets of bricks. Then there were two smaller vans and lots of people going backwards and forwards between them and the house. She wanted to get closer to see what was going on.

The road was in between her and the action, though, and she didn't like

the way the cars roared and growled
as they shot past. Yesterday, after a
few days of exploring the front garden,
she'd actually ventured out on to the
pavement. At first she'd just stood
by the gate, flinching back when a
car came past. But they all seemed to
stick to the road, and she was sure the
pavement looked safe enough.

She'd crept along the bottom of the
wall, keeping well away from the road.
Then a car had sped by. Cleo had felt
the rumbling of the road under her
paws and smelled the exhaust, and she'd
raced back to the safety of the garden.

She still wasn't quite brave enough
to cross the road and investigate the
unusual things that were happening
on the other side. Cleo edged between

two bushes as another van came driving up. But this time when the van stopped it was on *her* side of the road.

Cleo wriggled out between the thick stems, her whiskers twitching. The driver was getting out – Cleo could see his heavy boots walking round the side of the van. Then he opened up the back doors and lifted out a box, which he carried across the road to the interesting house on the other side.

Almost without realizing it, Cleo was padding eagerly out into the middle of the pavement. The van was new and exciting, and she wanted to see what was in it.

Then the man was coming back. Cleo ducked under the sprawling fuchsia bush in the garden next door.

Amber and Sara always tried to grab her when she went out at the front of the house. She didn't want this man to catch her now and stop her exploring. But the man didn't even notice her. He just unloaded another box and set off across the road again, leaving the van's back doors open.

As Cleo edged out of the bush, she came to a sudden halt. Her collar was caught on the wiry branches. She pulled at it crossly. She hated collars.

When the safety catch came open, she tossed her head briskly from side to side, enjoying the freedom. Then she hurried out from under the bush, shaking the dry leaves from her fur.

Cleo sniffed at the tyres of the van and then stretched up, putting her front paws on the little back step.

The van was full of boxes, some old sacks, a folded plastic sheet and all sorts of fascinating things. There were dark corners and good smells to investigate, too.

She jumped up, scrabbling to get her back legs on to the step, and clambered into the van. It was dusty, which made her sneeze, but that didn't put her off. She prowled further inside and rubbed up against one of the boxes. She liked this place and she wanted to mark it as hers.

Suddenly there was a shout from outside and the sound of footsteps approaching. Cleo froze, laying her ears back. What was happening? Was someone coming to chase her out? She backed between the box and a pile of sacks and watched, round-eyed, as the doors at the back of the van swung shut with a slam.

She was trapped.

# Chapter Three

Amber turned to her mum, smiling in relief. "It's OK! Cleo's not in the front garden. She must have decided to stay round the back today."

Mum nodded. "Maybe the novelty's worn off."

All the same, Amber was a little bit hurt that Cleo didn't come rushing to see her as she stepped into the house.

Whenever they'd been out over the summer holidays, she'd always come to greet them. As soon as she heard the door bang, she would come dashing downstairs from Amber's room, where she'd been asleep on her bed. Or sometimes she was sitting on the living-room windowsill, watching to see them drive up.

The house felt oddly quiet and empty without a little tortoiseshell cat twirling around her feet. "Cleo!" Amber called up the stairs. "Cleo, where are you?"

Mum pushed the front door shut and looked around in surprise. "Isn't she here? She's usually desperate for us to feed her when we get in from school."

"I know…" Amber said. "Cleo! Cleo!" She hurried through to the kitchen and out into the back garden. But no kitten came galloping over the grass to meet her. The garden was empty and still, with just a few birds twittering in the trees.

Amber trailed back inside, feeling worried.

Her mum was emptying one of Cleo's pouches of kitten food into her bowl and she glanced up as Amber came in. She put down the pouch, looking thoughtful. "No sign of her?" she asked.

Amber shook her head.

"That *is* odd. Go and check upstairs, Amber. She might have got shut in one of the bedrooms."

Amber smiled. "I didn't think about that! I hope she hasn't made a mess in Sara's room. Sara got really cross when Cleo tipped over all her hairbands and stuff the other day."

She raced upstairs, but all the bedroom doors were ajar. She checked the airing cupboard on the landing, just in case, but she wasn't in there... Or in Sara's wardrobe, or hers, or Mum and Dad's. She wasn't anywhere at all.

"Mum, I don't know where she can be," Amber said, bursting back into the kitchen. She was trying very hard not to cry. Mum would only say she was getting in a state about nothing. But this really didn't feel like nothing. Cleo never missed meals.

Mum put her arm round Amber's shoulders. "Sit down for a moment, have a drink, and let's think about this." She handed Amber some squash and pushed her gently into a chair. "Cleo was around just before lunch when I went into school. And we know she's been getting more adventurous lately, going over the wall into the front garden. She's probably just gone further than before. After all, you've only been back at school a week. Cleo doesn't really know what time you come home, does she? And the fact I'm working different times of day probably confuses her, too."

"I suppose so…"

"I expect she'll be back in a minute, yowling if we don't get her food in front of her before the cat flap bangs shut."

Amber tried to laugh, but she couldn't quite manage it.

Cleo stood perched on the pile of old sacks, mewing anxiously. She didn't understand why the doors had closed so suddenly. All she knew was that now she couldn't get out. She started to pick her way carefully between the boxes back towards the doors. Perhaps when she got closer she'd find a way to escape. When she pushed on doors in the house, sometimes they opened. Although sometimes they didn't... She scampered up to the doors and scrabbled at them with her front paws. They were shut tight.

There was a growling noise and then suddenly the van lurched, and Cleo slipped over sideways with a little squeak of fright. She'd only been in a car a few times, when she was brought home from the shelter and for trips to the vet. She'd always travelled in a comfortable basket, padded with a blanket, though. She slid across the floor of the van as it pulled out into the road, meowing frantically. She hadn't meant for this to happen at all.

Cleo pressed herself into a small dark space under a storage locker that had been built for tools. It was a tight fit, but it made her feel safer. Nothing could get at her under here. She squashed herself back against the cold metal of the van's wall and waited.

Eventually the van seemed to slow down, and then it lurched to a stop.

The noisy engine was turned off, leaving Cleo's ears buzzing. There was a crunching, clashing sound, and the doors swung open. Cleo wriggled her nose out of the tiny gap and tried to see what was happening. She could smell the fresh air coming in through the open doors, and she desperately wanted to race for them. But there was so much noise. She darted back into her safe hiding place as a huge box slid past her with a shriek of metal on metal and shivered. What if more of the boxes moved as she ran for the doors? She had to try, though.

Cleo laid her ears back close to her head and crept out. With her tummy pressed against the floor of the van, she edged across to the doors.

She could see the road outside, and
her whiskers twitched with the warm
smells of the sunny afternoon. But
just as she was getting ready to jump
down, the doors clanged shut. She was
trapped once more.

Cleo flung herself at the doors with
a desperate wail, banging her paws
against the hard metal. The doors
didn't budge. She should have run
for it when she could! Furious and
frightened, she stomped back across

the van, the fur all along her spine raised, her tail fluffed up. What was going to happen now? What if she never got out?

Miserably aware of how hungry and thirsty and lonely she felt, Cleo meowed as loudly as she could, hoping that Amber would come, the way she always did. *Surely* Amber would come and rescue her…

"Amber, I don't think she can have been hit by a car," Mum said gently, as Amber's dad came into the kitchen and hung his laptop bag over a chair. "We'd have heard. Cleo's microchipped. If she'd been taken to a vet, they would have called my mobile."

Amber had searched everywhere she could think of. She'd opened every cupboard in the house, remembering the day when Dad had accidentally shut Cleo in the cupboard under the stairs. And then she'd gone back and checked all the drawers, too. When Sara had got home from school, the sisters had gone down their road calling for her, while Mum had checked the garage and the shed. But Cleo was nowhere to be found. And what made it even worse was that Amber and Sara had found her collar under one of the bushes in front of the house next door. So now even if someone found her, they wouldn't know the number to call.

"What's up? Has Cleo disappeared?"
Dad asked, giving Amber a hug. "She's
probably just out exploring."

"Well, that's what I said," Mum
sighed. "But it's six o'clock, Dan.
She normally has her dinner about
four. It's really unusual for her not to
turn up for that."

"And now we've found her collar,"
Amber said shakily, pointing to it on
the kitchen table. "So we know she

was out at
the front of
the house.
What if
she's been
run over?"
"No,
your mum's

right. I'm sure someone would have found her and let us know, Amber." Dad frowned thoughtfully. "Maybe she is lost, though. She's only little – she could just have got confused about where she was going. How about I have another quick look along the street?"

When Dad came back a while later, he had to admit that he hadn't seen any sign of Cleo, either. As Amber picked at her dinner, she kept thinking of the open cat food pouch, which Mum had folded over and put in the fridge. Cleo must be so hungry, wherever she was.

"Try not to worry, Amber," Mum said, as she turned off Amber's light at bedtime. "She'll probably be back in the morning."

"You're not sure…"

Mum sighed. "No, I can't be *absolutely* sure. I really do think she will be, though."

Amber pulled the duvet over her head. She was desperate to sleep so that she could wake up and find Cleo stomping up and down her bed, purring and mewing until Amber got up and fed her her breakfast. But she lay awake for what seemed like hours, imagining the kitten hungry or lonely or, worst of all, hurt.

# Chapter Four

Cleo woke the next morning feeling stiff and cold. She had slept on the pile of sacks, but they weren't very comfortable, not compared to her soft basket. She was also desperately hungry. She had never gone for so long without a meal – or without Amber to stroke her and fuss over her and play with her.

She sat up, shaking out her paws, and

licked at the fur on her shoulders and neck. She felt so dusty and dirty in here. But washing only made her realize how much she needed a drink of water.

Cleo froze suddenly, with one paw lifted ready to sweep over her ear – she could hear footsteps. Someone was coming! She ducked behind a large crate and watched eagerly as the van doors swung open. Hands reached into the van and a box of tools clanked down loudly. Cleo edged forward. She crept round the boxes until she was just by the doors and waited for the footsteps to move further away again. Her heart was galloping – this was her chance!

Cleo jumped down on to the road and scurried under the van. She needed to stop and think about what to do next. She had hoped that once she was out of the van she would see her house, her garden wall and maybe even Amber. Although she knew that the van had moved, it had no windows in the back, and she didn't really understand that it had travelled from one place to another. So she was deeply confused when she realized that she was somewhere different – somewhere that did not smell familiar at all. Cleo peered out from round the back wheel of the van, looking up and down the road. She was lost.

Amber waved goodbye to Mum reluctantly and slung her rucksack over her shoulder. Lila came running up as she trailed into the playground.

"Are you all right?" Lila said anxiously. "Your eyes are all red. Amber, what's the matter?"

"It's Cleo," Amber sniffed. "She never came home for her tea last night. Mum and Dad said they were sure she'd be back when we got up, but she wasn't!" She swallowed hard. "I didn't want to come to school. I wanted to stay at home and keep looking for her. Mum said she's going to ring all the vets this morning. That's in case … in case she's been brought in because she's had an accident."

"Oh no," Lila whispered. "But you were saying only yesterday that you were worried about her being run over."

"I know!" Amber pressed her hands into her eyes. She didn't want to start crying again, not at school. "That makes it worse," she whispered. "I feel like I made it happen by worrying about it."

Lila put an arm round her shoulders. "Of course you didn't," she said firmly. "All it means is that you were sensible to worry. And you don't know that anything bad's happened! She might just be shut in somebody's garage."

"I guess so," Amber muttered.

Then Maisie came hurrying up, and Amber stared down at her shoes as

Lila whispered what had happened.
She didn't want to hear her friends
talking about it – it only made Cleo's
disappearance seem more real.

"Did you go
looking for her?"
Maisie asked.

"Down the whole
street. And Dad
asked some of the
neighbours when he
got home last night. If
Cleo isn't back by this
afternoon, we're going
to put posters up."

Lila made a face. "I hate those
posters. They're so sad. But I bet they
work," she added hurriedly.

"There's the bell." Maisie squeezed

Amber's hand. "Are you going to be OK? Do you want us to say something to Mr Evans for you?"

Amber shook her head, horrified. Imagine her teacher making a fuss and the whole class knowing. "I'll be fine. Please don't tell anyone, Maisie. I just don't want to talk about Cleo – it's making me feel too miserable."

After school, Amber dashed out to find her mum, hoping that she'd have good news. But she could tell as soon as she saw Mum on the other side of the playground that she didn't. She looked worried, even though she smiled at Amber and held out her arms for a hug.

57

"She hasn't come home, has she?" Amber asked, her voice muffled in her mum's jacket.

"Not yet, sweetie."

Amber swallowed. It felt like her heart was swelling up and blocking her throat. "Let's go home," she told Mum, and her voice sounded odd, even to her. "We need to start on the Lost Cat posters. I'll find a good photo of Cleo."

"Yes, I suppose we should," Mum agreed. "I really did think she'd have turned up by now. I wonder if she's shut in somewhere."

"Where?" Amber turned to look at Mum.

"Someone's shed, maybe? You know how nosy Cleo is. If she found one open she'd definitely pop in for a look around. And then maybe the person came back and shut the door without seeing her."

Amber nodded. "Oh, yes! I'll put that on the poster, then. We'll ask if people can look in their sheds. And Lila said she could be shut in a garage. I wonder if there's anywhere else…"

As soon as she got home, Amber raced upstairs to find the laptop she shared with Sara. Normally they argued about whose turn it was to have it, but Amber knew that today Sara wouldn't mind if she got it out of her bedroom. She carried it into her own room and started to work out what the poster should say.

"Amber?"

Amber gazed up at Sara in the doorway. "Look!" she sniffed, holding out the laptop to her big sister. There were tears dripping down her nose.

"Oh…" Sara sat down next to Amber on the bed, peering over at the photo on the screen. "I took that one on Mum's mobile. Cleo thought the phone was something she could eat – that's why she's so close up. She looks really cute."

"I bet she's really scared, wherever she is," Amber sobbed. "She's not going to understand what's going on, is she? She won't even know we're looking for her."

"I bet she will," Sara said. "She knows we love her, Amber. I'll help you put the posters up, and she'll be home soon. It'll be OK."

Once she'd darted out from under the van on to the pavement, Cleo squirmed under the nearest gate. She still had no idea where she was and why she couldn't find her way home to Amber, but she was so thirsty. She had to find something to drink.

She followed her nose down the pathway at the side of the house and came out into the back garden. She could smell water, she was sure. There was a delicate pattering sound and she hurried towards it. She was right – there was a huge bowl full of water, with a little fountain in the middle.

Cleo put her paws up on the edge and drank greedily. It tasted odd, not like the water from her bowl at home, but it was still good. She liked the fountain too, and she darted her head about, trying to catch the water drops in her mouth. They got on her ears and her whiskers, but she didn't mind – it helped to get rid of the dusty feeling.

Cleo padded across the garden, sniffing for something to eat – she felt much hungrier, now that she wasn't so thirsty. There was a definite smell of at least one other cat around, but none appeared.

Eventually she came to a little teepee set up on the grass. She peered around the tent flap, sniffing hopefully. There on a rug was a plastic plate, with half a stale sandwich on it. Cleo darted in and gobbled down the sandwich, which was full of dry cheese. It was delicious! She was still hungry, so she washed herself thoroughly all over, making sure she got every last crumb out of her whiskers.

Then she yawned and curled up on

the bit of the rug that was in the sun. The garden was quiet and felt safe, and the September sun was very warm. Before long Cleo was fast asleep.

She was woken mid-afternoon by a sudden noise – a loud wailing. Panicked, Cleo whisked round to the other side of the tent and hid behind it, peering out to see what was going on.

A boy came out of the back door of the house, carrying a plate. He wasn't the one making the noise – that seemed to be coming from inside. The boy wandered to the end of the garden and sat down on a swing beside the tent. He swung idly back and forth, nibbling at the sandwich. He was staring vaguely round the garden when he spotted Cleo.

He stopped swinging at once, and Cleo froze.

The boy slipped off the swing, leaving the sandwich on the grass and crept towards the tent.

"Here, puss, puss…" he called.

Cleo shrunk back behind the tent, as the wailing started up again.

The boy glanced towards the house. "Is that noise scary? It's just my little brother throwing a wobbly."

Cleo could tell from the boy's voice that he was friendly. And he had another of those sandwiches. Cleo came a little way out and eyed him hopefully.

"I haven't seen you before," the boy murmured. "I wonder who's got a new kitten? You haven't got a collar on, have you?" He looked carefully at the kitten's neck. "Nope, no collar. Hey, where are you going? Oh!" He laughed. The kitten was hurrying over the grass towards his abandoned sandwich. "Do you want it? Oh, wow, you do."

Cleo was already tearing at the corner of the sandwich, gulping it down greedily.

"You're starving!" The boy smiled slowly as he watched the sandwich disappear. "Maybe you're a stray?"

He grinned as the kitten devoured the last bit of sandwich and sniffed the plate all over to see if she'd missed any.

"Who do you belong to, hey? What's your name?" He reached out to tickle Cleo gently behind the ears. "I reckon you look like a … umm. Maybe a Smudge? With that dark splodge over your eye? But you look like a girl cat to me. Smudge doesn't sound like a girl. What about Patch? Are you called

Patch? That's why my mum called our cat Pirate, you know. Because he's got an eyepatch."

"George! George!"

Cleo darted away behind the tent again, and the boy sighed. "There's Mum. I'll come back later with some more food for you. That's if you're still here…"

# Chapter Five

Amber followed Sara back into the house, trying to feel hopeful. They had put up posters all along their street and the streets close by. Then they'd gone into the little convenience store at the end of their road and asked if they could put up one on their notice board. But it still didn't feel like enough. Amber couldn't just sit in the house, waiting for Cleo to come home. She needed to be doing something.

Perhaps she could go and ask some of their neighbours who had sheds and garages if she could check them. Then her eyes widened – she'd just thought of another place where Cleo could have got trapped. The family across the road was having a lot of work done on their house and had moved in with their grandparents for a few weeks. Jan, their mum, had told Amber's mum that they'd have to pack everything up in boxes. But that meant some of the rooms were closed up, and there were piles of stuff everywhere – all sorts of places where a kitten could get shut in.

Amber was so excited, and so sure

she was right, that she didn't even stop to ask Mum or Sara to go with her. She'd just have time to catch the builders before they went home, she reckoned. She slipped back out of the front door and crossed the road. Mum would tell her off, but if she came back with Cleo, surely Mum wouldn't mind that much… And Amber was certain she would bring her back.

She hesitated outside number 22, looking for one of the builders to ask. Until now, every time they'd gone past there had been someone around, unloading stuff from vans or hoisting materials up on to the scaffolding. But now there was no one at all.

"Hello?" Amber called, stepping on to the driveway.

No one came. Amber clenched her fists. She just couldn't wait any longer. What if Cleo was starving? She knew it was stupid – and she'd get into trouble if Mum and Dad found out she'd gone into Jan's garden with all the building going on. But she had to!

She walked up to the house and tried to peer in through the front windows, pressing her nose against the glass. She was trying so hard to see through the dusty panes that she didn't hear one of the builders coming round the side of the house.

"Just what exactly do you think you're doing?"

Amber swung round to find a tall man staring down at her. He was covered in dust. The greyish colour made him look like a statue. "I'm – I'm looking for my kitten," she squeaked.

"Your *kitten*?"

"She's gone missing. I thought she might have got shut in…" Amber's voice trailed away – the man looked so cross.

"You shouldn't be here. Don't you realize how dangerous it is, messing around on a building site?"

Amber hung her head, tears filling her eyes. Then she looked up again, straightening her shoulders. This was too important to let go. "But she's been gone a whole day. What if she's got trapped somewhere? Jan said some of the rooms were shut up to keep the dust out – what if she's in one of them?"

"They've all been closed up since we started," the man said, more gently. "And we'd have heard her mewing, wouldn't we?"

Amber's head drooped again. "Maybe… I really thought she had to be here.  I'm so worried about her."

"I'll keep an eye out for her," the man told Amber. "What colour is she?"

"She's a tortoiseshell, mostly gingery with black patches. We live just there." Amber pointed across the road.

"All right. Now, out of here, and don't even think of coming back. What if something had fallen off the scaffolding?"

Amber nodded, her eyes widening. She hurried out of the garden and crossed the road, her cheeks burning. That had been awful. But at least the builder hadn't insisted on coming back home with her and telling Mum.

George slid back through the kitchen, glad that his mum was still occupied sorting out Toby, his little brother. Everyone said that Toby was going through a stage, or that it was the terrible twos, but it basically meant that he was either really, really happy or furious and never anything in between. Right now it meant that Mum wasn't going to notice him sneaking his leftover packed lunch outside to the kitten.

George checked – yes, there was quite a bit of his lunch left. He didn't think the kitten would be keen on grapes, but she would definitely be up for cocktail sausages, he decided. Pirate was always trying to nick them when Mum was making his packed lunch.

He hurried back down the garden, hoping that the kitten would still be there. *Perhaps I should really be hoping that she's gone home*, George thought to himself, feeling a bit guilty. The little kitten was probably still not used to being out much.

Then he saw her peeping at him from behind the tent again and forgot to worry about her owner.

As soon as Cleo saw the boy, she darted out from her hiding place at once and came up quite close. Maybe he had more food. She still felt so hungry, even after both those sandwiches. She was used to two good meals and the odd snack of cat treats from Amber. She stopped a short distance away and sniffed at the lunchbox as George put it down on the grass.

George held out a sausage on the palm of his hand and looked hopefully at the kitten. Then he laughed as the little cat dived at him and started  nibbling the sausage straight out of his hand. Her mouth was so soft, and her damp nose nuzzled at George's fingers.

"You're really nice," he whispered, using his not-sausagey hand to stroke the kitten's soft back.

The kitten finished off the sausage and looked hopefully into the lunchbox for more. She snagged the last sausage out of the little pot, and it disappeared in seconds.

"Don't make yourself sick," George told her. "Sorry, that's the last one. There's still a bit of cheese, though." He took it out and pulled off the cling film. "There you go." He watched, smiling, as the kitten ate the cheese, too, and then sat down quite heavily and began to wash her ears and face. Her stomach looked a lot rounder than it had ten minutes ago.

"I wish I knew where you'd come from, Patch," George murmured. "I probably shouldn't have given you all that food, if you're just going to go home for your tea. But you looked starving, the way you wolfed down that sandwich."

The kitten licked her bright pink tongue over her nose and then looked at the boy with gleaming golden eyes. She got up and padded a little closer.

George gazed down in surprise – he'd thought maybe the kitten would hurry away once the food had all gone. But instead she clambered on to George's lap and slumped down, clearly exhausted by so much eating. She yawned, and then she seemed to melt into the space on George's lap, completely saggy, like a beanbag toy. She was asleep.

# Chapter Six

Cleo padded up to the shed and
wriggled through a small gap in the
boards. She gazed around, hoping to
find something else to eat. The boy,
George, had left her some food there
in the morning – toast crusts and the
end of a boiled egg. It wasn't like
anything Cleo had eaten before, but
she'd quite enjoyed it. She was feeling

hungry again
now, though.

George had
shown her this
place the evening
before. He'd opened the door and gone
in to shake the dust and spiders' webs
off some cushions from the garden
chairs. He had arranged them into a
comfy pile for a bed and filled an old
plant saucer from the outside tap with
water. He'd even brought Cleo a fish
finger. It was a bit fluffy from being in
his pocket, but she hadn't cared. Then
he'd shown Cleo that there was a hole
in the shed wall, just big enough for a
kitten to squeeze in and out of.

Cleo had spent the night curled up
on the cushions, but she kept startling

awake. It wasn't like being in a house. There were strange noises, and they seemed so close with just the thin wooden walls of the shed to protect her. Squeaks and chirrups and rustlings in the trees and the flowerbeds, and once, horribly close, a great deep sniff. Cleo had frozen, watching the little hole in the shed wall. After the sniff there had been a pause, a terrifying silence while she'd wondered if the creature was going to claw its way in. But it had gone away, obviously deciding that Cleo wasn't worth the effort. It had left behind a sharp, unmistakeable whiff of something wild, and hungry.

She had spent the day exploring the garden – every so often coming up against that smell again. She could still catch a trace of it now…

Cleo hated the thought of spending another night in the shed, with that creature so close by. As kind as George was, she needed to find her home, where she slept indoors on Amber's bed or occasionally in her basket. She wanted Amber to snuggle up against. She clambered back out of the shed then crept uncertainly past the house, down the side passage and out into George's front garden. There she looked out on to the street, wondering how to get home. It was mid-afternoon and quite quiet, even though there were children's voices in the distance, returning home from school. Cleo peered down the road hopefully, wondering if one of them was Amber, coming to find her. But the voices didn't sound right.

Cleo hopped up on to the wall, so she could look around from a high point. The street stretched out in front of her – grey and empty, and utterly unfamiliar. Which way should she go?

She sniffed the air, trying to catch a scent of home, but there was nothing. At last she jumped down from the wall and set off down the street, making for a garden with straggly bushes spilling out on to the pavement. She would go in short hops, from hiding place to hiding place, she decided. In case that creature was still around.

A strange rattling sound suddenly came around the corner of the road,

and Cleo scuttled towards the bushes
and ducked underneath. There was a
loud clattering and then footsteps. A
face appeared under the branches, and
Cleo's heart slowed a little. It was the
boy who had looked after her.

"What are you doing?" George
muttered. "You shouldn't be out on
the pavement – I bet you don't
understand about cars."

He thought
of Amber
at school,
worrying about
her kitten
getting run over.

He ought to ask her if the kitten had
been out in her front garden again.
She'd been really quiet at school today,

not at all chatty like she usually was.

He scooped Cleo up and snuggled her with one arm, glancing back over his shoulder. His mum hadn't got round the corner yet – Toby was throwing a strop about being in the pushchair.

"Don't wriggle too much," George warned. "It's tricky scooting with only one hand."

He whooshed the last few metres towards his house and shoved his scooter into the little shelter down the side passage. The man next door, Luke, had helped Dad build it for all their bikes and things. The kitten was wriggling more and more. "I know," he whispered. "I'm just waiting for Mum to open the door. Here, look!" He slipped his rucksack off his shoulders and crouched down, bringing out his lunchbox.

The kitten stopped struggling at once and pricked her ears forward.

"I saved you some of my lunch," George told her. "You like cheese, don't you?" He held out a cheese cube to the kitten, who swallowed it almost whole and then tried to burrow into the lunchbox to get more. George giggled. "You really do like cheese…" He peered round the corner of the side passage. "Just putting my scooter away, Mum!"

"All right. Close the front door when you come in," his mum called back. "Come on, Toby. We're home now."

"You see," George whispered. "Mum's still busy with my brother. She isn't going to notice if I sneak you up to my room, is she? You'll be safe up there, Patch. No more going near the road."

He picked up the lunchbox again, then hurried in through the front door and slipped upstairs.

"Can I make some leaflets about Cleo, Mum?" Amber asked, as she undid her school shoes. "Maisie suggested it. We could put them through people's doors, in case they didn't see the posters."

"I suppose it could encourage the neighbours to look in their sheds and garages," Mum agreed. "But you're not to go out delivering them without me or Sara," she added with a stern look.

Mum had been really cross the day

before, when Amber had come back in after going to the house across the road. Luckily, Amber hadn't had to explain exactly where she had been – she'd just said that she'd gone out looking for Cleo.

Amber opened up the laptop and started to write the leaflet. She dropped in the photo of Cleo and added a message asking people to check their sheds and garages, then put her mum's phone number at the bottom. Then she printed them out and went into the kitchen to show Mum.

"Do you want to go and deliver them now?" Mum asked. "I've got some time before I make dinner."

"Please." Amber hugged her. "Look, I've made enough for our road and

Bramble Crescent. Cleo could have easily gone round into their gardens."

Mum nodded and got out her phone. "I'll just text Sara to tell her where we are."

They set off down their road, taking turns to post the leaflets. It was surprisingly hard to push the flimsy sheets of paper through the letterboxes, and Amber hoped they wouldn't just get squashed inside and missed.

They were halfway back down the other side of the road when Amber noticed that the builder who'd told her off was coming out of Jan's house. She stopped, staring at him in panic. What if he told Mum about yesterday? Mum would be so cross. She posted the next few leaflets extra-slowly, hoping that he'd go back inside before they reached him. But he didn't.

As they approached the house, Amber lurked behind Mum. Maybe the builder would think that this was another family looking for their lost cat. But she was pretty sure he knew exactly who she was.

"Hello!" Mum smiled at him. "We're from across the road. Our kitten's gone missing. Can I give you one of these,

just in case you spot her? It's got my
number on. She's been gone a couple
of days now. Amber here's really
missing her."

Amber's eyes widened in panic. Now
he was bound to say something…

"Of course," the builder said. "Do you want to hand me a couple more? I can give them to the other guys. I'm Luke, by the way." He smiled at Amber, and she wasn't sure, but she thought he gave her just a hint of a wink, as if to say he'd keep her secret.

# Chapter Seven

"This is my bedroom," George
explained to the kitten. Then he
laughed to himself. "I know you don't
really understand a word I say," he
murmured. "You're more bothered
about the cheese than anything else,
aren't you? Here…" He grabbed a
piece of paper from his desk and used
it like a plate for his leftover sandwich.

"I can't keep on giving you sandwiches," he said. "It can't be good for you to be living on my leftovers. But Mum would have seen me if I got you some of Pirate's cat food."

He sat there watching the kitten nibble her way through the sandwich. He hadn't thought about keeping the kitten before. But could he? Of course the kitten might have a proper home where someone wanted her, even if she didn't have a collar. Some cats just wouldn't wear them. Pirate was an expert at taking

them off – or he had been. They used
to have to go on collar hunts in the
garden, but Pirate didn't go out much
any more. He was fourteen, and his legs
hurt. He spent most of his days asleep
on someone's bed. George really loved
him, but Pirate had always seemed
more like Mum's cat. He didn't play
with George that much. Not like this
bouncy little kitten… She could be his
very own.

"You've been in my garden a whole
day now," George pointed out. "At
least, I think you have. And you
haven't tried to go home. Do you
like it better here, Patch, hmm?" But
that didn't mean the kitten hadn't got
an owner… Maybe she was just good
at losing collars, too. George sighed.

She didn't really look like she had been living as a stray for a long time. She wasn't skinny or grubby-looking. "I expect someone's looking for you," he admitted. "Well, if you were mine, I'd be making a lot more effort to find you. I reckon you'd be better off with me."

The kitten gazed around George's bedroom with interest and padded over to investigate his bookcase. She gazed up at it, wriggled her bottom a bit and made a flying leap up to the top. Then she stood there looking proud of herself.

Cleo sniffed at George's Lego spaceship, and the fur rose a little along her spine. She liked this house, and she liked the boy. But there was something wrong. Cleo hadn't shared a home with another cat since she left the shelter where she'd lived with her mother and the rest of her litter, but she was almost sure there was another cat here. That this house *belonged* to another cat. And perhaps the boy belonged to the other cat, too.

She nosed at the spaceship again, leaping back a little as it slid away on its wheels, and the boy leaped to catch it. Then Cleo jumped down again and wandered over to George's bed. The other-cat smell was even stronger here. She backed away from the bed, her tail twitching nervously.

Just then the bedroom door swung open and the boy jumped. "Oh, Pirate, it's only you! I thought it was Mum. Hey, don't be like that…"

A huge black-and-white cat stood in the doorway, glaring at Cleo. His fat black tail was slowly fluffing up, getting even fatter as every hair stood on end. Pirate hissed, lowering his head to stare Cleo in the eyes.

Cleo felt her own fur rising up and she hissed, too – a thin, feeble noise compared to the sound the larger cat was making.

"Oh no," George muttered. The kitten was crouched by his bed, looking terrified – but her tail was switching from side to side in just the same angry way that Pirate's was.

"Pirate, she's just a kitten." He got up and tried to shoo Pirate out of his room, but Pirate wasn't having any of it. He swerved round George and jumped at the smaller cat, sending her flying with a fat paw.

"No!" George yelled, panicking. He'd never expected this to happen. Pirate was so slow and sleepy, but now it was like he'd got ten years younger. Pirate was massive compared to the kitten – what if he really hurt the little thing? George reached down, trying to grab the kitten. He'd go and put her in

the garden and shut Pirate in. But then
he jumped back with a yelp. He'd got
in between Pirate and the kitten, and
there were claw marks all down the
back of his hand, oozing thin red lines
of blood.

George looked miserably at Pirate
– he'd never seen him look so furious.
But he supposed he should have
realized. This was Pirate's house, and
another cat had suddenly turned up.
Pirate was right to be hissing and
spitting and clawing. Then he gasped
as Pirate launched himself at the
kitten, bowling her over with a swipe
from his huge paw.

Cleo squealed in fright. This was
nothing like the play fights she'd had
with her brothers and sisters back at

the shelter, and she didn't know what to do. She made a desperate leap, scrabbling on to the windowsill.

Pirate sat below, staring up at Cleo, still making those horrible hissing sounds – but he couldn't easily jump to that height any more.

Cleo didn't know that, though. The window was only open a crack, but she just managed to shoot through the gap before George could grab her.

"Come back!" George wailed. His bedroom was at the side of the house, and the window looked out on to the two garages – theirs and next door's. The kitten was teetering on the narrow windowsill.

"Come on, here, puss," George called. He was trying to sound calm and coaxing, but his voice was trembling. The kitten hissed at him and jumped down on to the steeply sloping garage roof. She clung to the tiles, her fur all fluffed up and her eyes round with fear.

George raced out of his bedroom and almost crashed into his mum on the landing.

"George? What's going on? What was all that noise? Are you teasing Pirate?"

"No! I'll explain in a minute." He dodged past his mum, tore down the stairs and out of the front door.

"Please come down," George whispered, gazing up at the kitten. "I really don't want you to fall."

His mum appeared at the door,

looking really cross. "George! What is going on? Get back in here!"

"I can't, Mum. Look…" He pointed up at the kitten, and his mum came over to see.

"Oh!" Mum cried. "Whose kitten is that?"

"I don't know. But she's stuck on the roof." George felt bad not explaining how the kitten had got on to the roof in the first place, but he hadn't exactly told his mum a lie…

"How on earth are we going to get it down?" Mum said. "Poor little thing – it looks terrified!"

"Kitty!" Toby clambered down the front step and pointed up at the kitten.

Mum caught his hand quickly. "Yes, it is. But the kitty's stuck, Toby. Shh, now, don't scare it."

"Mum, what are we going to do?" George whispered.

"Pirate!" His mum gasped, pointing up at George's window. "How did he get up there?"

George craned his neck to look

up at the window. He could just see Pirate's black-and-white face, pressed up against the opening. But Pirate was too big to squeeze through the way the kitten had. He just stood there, yowling.

Cleo could see him, too. The older cat looked enormous, and she was sure it was about to leap out of the window after her. She backed away, hissing, but her claws slipped on the tiles, and she slid even further down the steep roof with a terrified mew.

Mum turned to George. "We need a ladder. There's one in the shed – at least, I think there is… Stay here with Toby and try to calm the kitten down. First I'm going to get Pirate off there before he hurts himself or frightens the little one even more." She pushed Toby's hand into George's and disappeared inside.

George looked up at the kitten clinging desperately on to the roof and felt so guilty. He should never have brought her into the house.

"Just hold on," he called softly. "It's going to be OK. We'll get you down. And then I promise we'll try and find who you really belong to."

# Chapter Eight

"Are you all right?" said a man's voice from behind George.

George whirled round. It was Luke from next door. George hadn't even heard his van drive up. "Hi!" he said breathlessly. "Do you have a ladder in your van? Mum's gone to look for one, but she's not sure where it is."

"What do you need a ladder... Oh,

I see." Luke peered up at the kitten clinging to the garage roof. "Hold on a sec." He hurried back to his van.

George went back to murmuring nonsense to the kitten and trying to stop Toby from climbing up the drainpipe to get to her. He glanced up at his bedroom. Mum must have grabbed Pirate and put him somewhere safe, because now his window was wide open. Maybe Mum thought the kitten could jump back in. But George was pretty sure such a little cat couldn't jump up there from the steep roof, not without sliding back down again.

"I've shut Pirate in the kitchen," said his mum, rushing out. "But I can't find the ladder, I think it must be in the garage."

"It's OK." George pointed to Luke, who was coming up the path with a stepladder. "Luke's got one."

His mum gave a huge sigh of relief. "Hi, Luke. You turned up just at the right time. I've got a bag of cat treats. I was thinking we could try and coax the kitten back up to the window with them, but it'll definitely be easier this way."

Luke unfolded the ladder and slowly moved it towards the garage. "I don't want to scare it away," he said. "Pass me some of those treats."

Mum emptied a few into his hand and he climbed up the ladder, holding out the treats towards the kitten. "Come on, puss. Here, look. Don't you want them?"

Cleo hissed feebly at the strange man.

She was so frightened she didn't know what to do – she could only cling on.

George watched, his heart thumping. What if Luke couldn't reach? Or the kitten tried to dodge him and fell?

"Hold the ladder, can you?" Luke called down quietly to George's mum. "I need both hands… Aha! Got you." The kitten wriggled in his arms as he climbed back down the ladder one-handed. "There we are. You're safe now. Yes, you eat those."

He laughed as Cleo sniffed out the cat treats at last, leaning over to nuzzle eagerly at the bag in George's mum's hand. "Well, it doesn't look like she's come to any harm, does it?" He peered at Cleo's black and white and ginger coat, frowning. "I wonder… But it's too far, surely. Here, can you hold her a minute?" Luke passed the kitten to George and dug in his pocket. "Would you say she looks like that?" He held out a slip of paper, with a little photo of a kitten on it.

"Yes," George's mum said, looking at the leaflet. "I think so…"

"I don't believe it." Luke shook his head. "Well, that girl who lives opposite the house I'm working on is going to be pleased, if this really is her. Are you Cleo, hey?"

"Cleo!" George gasped. He stared at the kitten. "*Amber's* Cleo?"

Luke looked thoughtful. "I think her mum did say she was

called Amber. She's got red hair?"

"That's her! This is Amber's cat? She's in my class. So that's why she's been looking so upset." He looked down at Cleo, his cheeks reddening. He'd wanted to steal Amber's kitten! "But how did she get all the way over here?" he asked suddenly. "Amber told me she lives on the other side of town, by the adventure playground."

Luke made a face and nodded towards the van. "Well, guess where that's been parked. Right outside her house."

"Amber did say her kitten was really nosy," George said. "She was worried about her getting run over, because she'd started going out on to the street."

"You think she got into your van?" George's mum said in surprise, shaking out a few more cat treats and feeding them to Cleo.

"She must have done. I'd better take her home," Luke sighed. "And apologize for catnapping her."

"You didn't mean to!" George's mum laughed. "I'm sure they'll just be delighted to have her back. Do you want to borrow Pirate's cat carrier? The poor kitten probably won't like it much, it'll smell of Pirate, but you'll need to put her in something."

"Before she eats all the cat treats and makes a getaway!" Luke agreed.

"Can I come with you?" George asked shyly. "I won't get in the way or anything. I'd just like to help take her home."

"If it's OK with your mum. You can

sit in the front with me and hold the carrier. I don't want it wobbling about."

"Of course you can," Mum said. "Hold on a minute and I'll get it out of the garage."

George smiled. He could imagine how pleased Amber was going to be. If he'd lost Pirate, he'd have been in a real state.

"Amber, can you get the door?" Mum called. "I've got crumble mix all over my hands."

Amber put down the jingly ball she'd found under the shoe rack, blinking away her tears. She kept wanting to cry – everything in the house seemed to remind her of Cleo.

"If it's those window people again, just say no thank you," her mum added.

Amber's mum really didn't like people trying to sell her double-glazing, and they always turned up when she was cooking the dinner. Amber opened the front door, rehearsing a polite go-away smile.

"Oh!" It was the builder from across the road. Amber bit at her bottom lip. What if he was coming to tell Mum on her, after all? But he was smiling.

"I've brought you a present. Me and my friend here." He stepped back so that Amber could see the boy beside him, who was holding a plastic cat carrier.

"George?" Amber stared at her classmate for a moment – then she looked down at the cat carrier, and her eyes went wide with hope. "Have you… Have you—?"

"Is it her?" George asked anxiously. "We thought it must be."

Cleo scrabbled madly at the sides of the carrier, mewing and mewing. Amber was there! The boy had brought her back to Amber. Why wouldn't they let her out?

"Amber, what is it?" Amber's mum came up the hallway, drying her hands on a tea towel. "Luke, hello. Is there a problem over the road?"

"Mum, they've found Cleo! Thank you so much!" Amber pulled open the latch and reached in to stroke the kitten. "I thought you'd never come home…" she murmured, lifting her out and snuggling Cleo against her shoulder.

"Where was she?" she asked.

"I found her in my garden," George explained. "But I didn't know she was yours. I, um, fed her my leftovers," he admitted. "And then she got stuck on our garage roof, and Luke helped to get her down." He couldn't bring himself to tell Amber that he'd lured her kitten into his house and got her into a fight with Pirate.

But Amber beamed at him. "Thank you for feeding her. I was so worried she was going to be starving!"

"I reckon she went for a ride in the back of my van," Luke put in. "I can't see how else she turned up in our neighbourhood. It's a good couple of miles away."

"Goodness," Amber's mum said.

"She stowed away! I'll have to ring Sara and Dad and tell them. You don't know how relieved they'll be. We were imagining the worst things…"

"I'm glad I found her," George said to Amber.

"Not as glad as I am," Amber said, giggling as Cleo licked her chin. "You couldn't be."

"You know a lot about cats," Amber said admiringly, watching George tickle Cleo on just the right spot behind her ear. She'd invited George round to tea to say thank you – and to let him see how Cleo was. He'd asked Amber about her at school a few times, and she thought George must have really liked the kitten.

"Our cat's called Pirate, because he looks like he has an eye patch. He's my mum's actually. She got him before I was born."

"So he's pretty old then?"

"Uh-huh. He's a bit slow now – he doesn't race around like this one does. But he's still special," George added firmly.

It was true. Pirate might be slow and not that good at chasing toys, but he almost always slept on George's feet at night. Mum had told him the other night that Pirate had done that since George was a baby. She and Dad had tried to keep him away because they were worried that Pirate might hurt him by accident. But Pirate wouldn't be shooed away – and he was the best one for stopping baby George crying. "In the end we gave up," his mum had said, smiling down at Pirate, who was sitting between them. "He'd obviously decided you were his, you see."

George watched Cleo clamber up into Amber's lap and flop down, purring. He stroked her ears, and nodded to himself. Amber was Cleo's, and he belonged to Pirate – and that was exactly the way it should be.

**Out Now:**

Sammy the Shy Kitten

From best-selling author HOLLY WEBB

Out Now:

The
Seaside
Puppy

From best-selling author
HOLLY WEBB